W9-ABS-612

are you
listening?

tillie walden

are you listening?

New York

Published by First Second
First Second is an imprint of Roaring Brook Press,
a division of Holtzbrinck Publishing Holdings Limited Partnership
120 Broadway, New York, NY 10271

Don't miss your next favorite book from First Second!
For the latest updates go to firstsecondnewsletter.com and sign up for our enewsletter.

Library of Congress Control Number: 2018953552

Paperback ISBN: 978-1-250-20756-2
Hardcover ISBN: 978-1-62672-773-1

Our books may be purchased in bulk for promotional, educational, or business use.
Please contact your local bookseller or the Macmillan Corporate and Premium Sales Department
at (800) 221-7945 ext. 5442 or by email at MacmillanSpecialMarkets@macmillan.com.

First edition, 2019

Edited by Connie Hsu
Book design by Molly Johanson
Printed in China

Paperback: 10 9 8 7 6 5 4 3 2 1
Hardcover: 10 9 8 7 6 5 4 3 2 1

DRIPPING SPRINGS
AUSTIN
DEL RIO
DUBLIN
SAN ANTONIO
BIG SPRING
MARFA
EL PASO
HOUSTON
LUCKENBAC
SAN ANGELO
PARIS
MIDLAND
GRUENE
PORT ARANSAS
DALLAS
FORT STOCKTON
AMARILLO
BELLAIRE
MUENSTER
The guidebooks play deception; oceans are
A property of mind. All maps are fiction,
All travelers come to separate frontiers.
–Adrienne Rich,
"Itinerary"

HOUSTON

2014

creeaaakkk

you gettin' on?

Kid?

no. no, sorry.
Suit yourself

fuck

really?

HONK

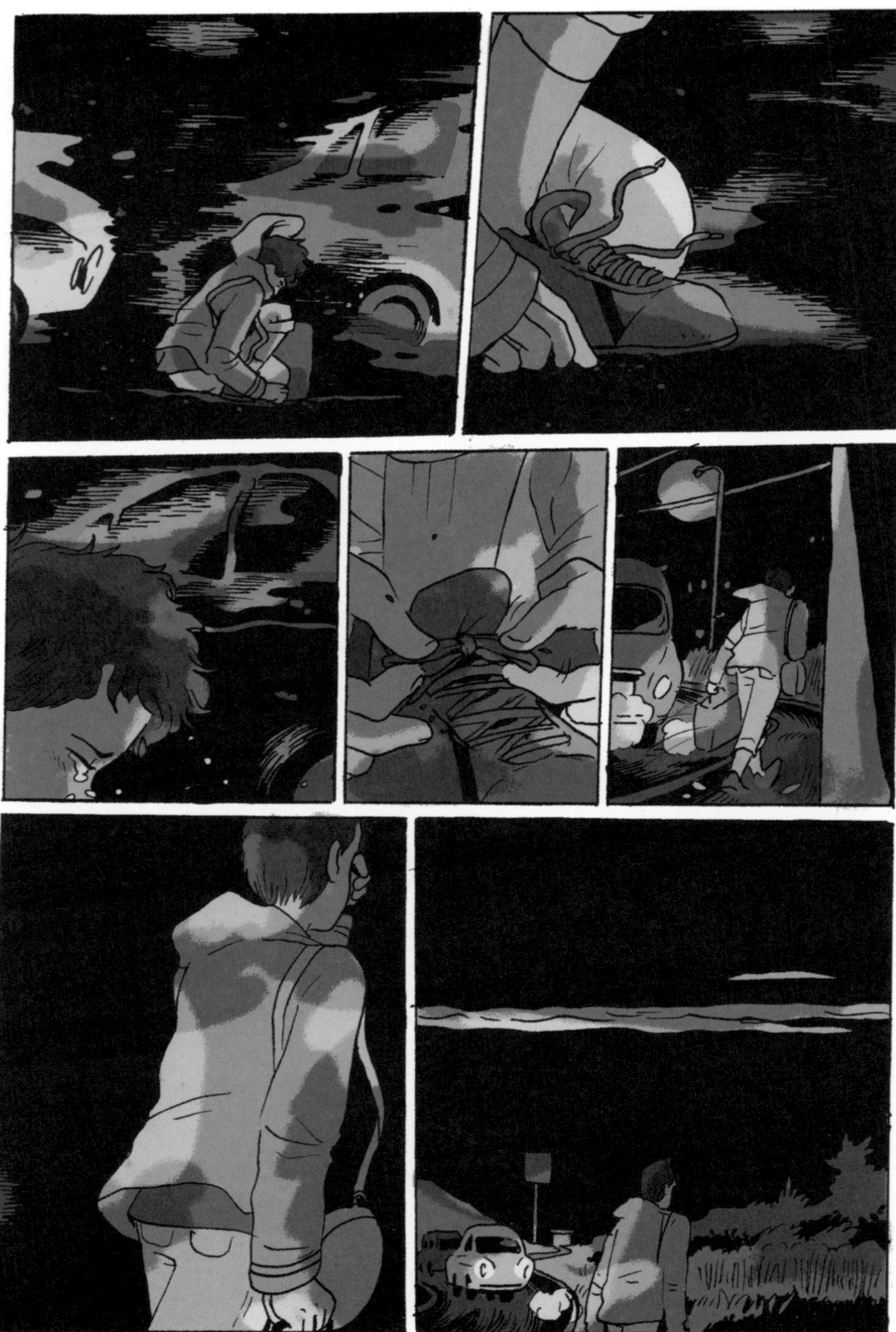

what am
I doing?

SAN ANGELO

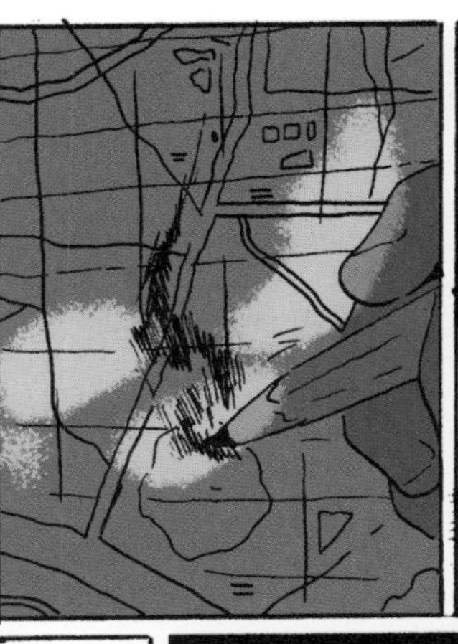

HONK

HRNK

BEEP

HOOO

HONK

shit

BRKK

NNNK

HONK

why is everyone STOPPED? Lord...

now I'm fucking wet...

OK, OK, OK

LUCKY'S
GAS · FOOD

COLA
COFFEE
ICE

BIG SPRING
MIDLAND
WEST
DING

I ♡ TEXAS
JESUS
excuse me

TEXAS FOREVER
BIG SPRING
Um, excuse me, do you have a phone? I...
DING
y'all got a bathroom?
BEAUTY

the bathroom is for customers ***only***.
lord

uh... ok, lemme get...
this gum.

DING
Whaddya need, Kid?

Kid?
Oh, uh...

nothing, I'm fine, I—
Beatrice?

it's Beatrice, right? Lin's kid?

yeah
What on god's green earth are you doing way out here?

I... uh, nothing. I have to go, actually.
ma'am
you like gum?
what?
gum.
I guess
ma'am
I hate the stuff—it's all yours.
makes my mouth itch.
ma'am
MA'AM.
YES
your bathroom key
thank you
wow

I haven't seen you since-
I gotta run
oh
ok
wait, are you out here alone?
ma'am
what
you need to use the key right away so it's available for other customers.
no one else is here.
DING
I'm going, I'm going...
god

VISIT
ODESSA
FISHIN
SWIMMIN
EATIN
euch

THE WITCH
FUN GUM
MADE IN MCKINN

DING

DING

Hey!
wait!

Hey, um.. I—
I'm sorry, I'm...
your name...
Lou

Lou! Right. I knew that.
Lou
you–
I–
oh, sorry
no, go ahead
um
I... I missed my bus and I don't think there's another...
where you headed?
what?
Oh, uh...
Mckinney
Mckinney?
Yeah. I... have a friend there.
I don't think it's too far. Besides, I owe your mom after she helped me clear that dead tree last month.
really? you'll–
Sure.
As long as you don't try to steal my car again.

hah

can you pass me that map?

where are you going?

me? Oh... just out west, see some family.
a short trip.

Why are you driving this late...?
Just...uh... because... I...
I didn't ask you why you're running away.
running, I'm NOT-
Oh, come on. Do your parents know you're out here?

I... I'm not... I'm 18, not 12. I can leave home if I want to.
that's what I thought.
seriously? I help you out and you're gonna scream at me? I don't need this shit
then pull over. Drop me off.
I'm obviously not gonna do that.

you're wrong.
What?
I was... only 15 then...
I wasn't gonna steal your car.
that's not what I was doing.

can I roll down the window?
sure

So... you got in my car to..?
I just wanted to sit in it. I don't even know how to drive.

you have a million cars. I didn't think you'd notice.

and if you had known how to...

I would've taken off. Never looked back.

I knew it.

My mom taught me to drive. I must've been... god, 10, maybe?
I was driving her old truck in this bumpy field by our house...
It was so hard trying to shift and steer over rocks and holes.
and then a few years later she got this car.
it was so shiny and new it looked like it came from space.
you got to drive it?
not at first. But we took our first road trip in it.
I was so nervous that I would scratch it, break something...
and within the first hour I spilled my hot chocolate everywhere.
no way
you can still see the stain.

I thought I was gonna get in so much trouble
you didn't?
nope. She started laughing. Told me then and there that this car was gonna be mine someday.
Stains and all.
it's strange driving it without her.
if I'm not thinking I still go to the passenger side.
I'm sorry... I heard, I mean... about...
Can you roll up the window?

Why didn't you learn to drive? Every kid in town seems to be barreling around in some rusty pickup.
and I'm always the one fixing it when they drive into a ditch...
I know you have a car, I worked on your mom's—
I just never learned.
Why does it even matter?
fine, fine. Forget I asked.

I was gonna learn to drive.

My mom said she'd teach me on my 16th birthday.

But... my little brother got sick. She was with him all day.
I still waited by the car for her, just in case.

She-
She forgot.

You couldn't learn... another time?
I didn't want to learn another time.

It's late. You can close your eyes if you need to.
we're still a good hour away
what time is it?
Just past 2 a.m.

Beatrice

we're 20 minutes away.
YAWN

what?
from McKinney
oh
right

that was quick

MCKINNEY
25 MILES

thanks for...
you know.
thanks
Lou?
Lou! Why are
we stopping?
Lou?

push the clutch in
I am
I think.
all the way to the floor. There you go.
right foot on the accelerator... no, that's the brake...
there you go
what do I do?

relax.
we're in first gear. You're gonna slowly let out the clutch...
slowly let out...
While you push on the accelerator.
push on the...

clutch
accelerator
crk
AHH
don't worry
that sounded bad
it's fine
you let the clutch out too fast.
I did not
try again
slowly
slowly...

CRRKKK
too fast
Why are you laughing?
because it's 3 a.m.
I'm perfectly awake.
try again
clutch...
accelerator...
try again
UGH

don't feel bad; it takes practice.
MCKINNEY 5 MILES
I know

is it true you built a whole car when you were 13?

that's what I heard
I need to look at the map.
it isn't true?
I was 15

that's so cool
it's really not
it totally is

it was cool when it was just my mom being proud...
and when I got to see that I had this... talent

But now it's a story people in town tell.
now it's something else.

do you have an address?
are you really just going to visit family?

what?

shoes

this is a lot of stuff for a short—
where am I dropping you off?

uh, up here is fine.
here?

I'll... I mean,
she lives close.
I'll find it.

you don't have
an address?
I have it
somewhere.

So, I'll see you.
I guess.
thanks

goddamn

there is
no friend,
is there?

I'll be fine.
wait, where are you going to sleep?

do you even know anyone in McKinney?

no.
then... why are we here?

it was on the gum.
the...
the gum.

from the gas station.

BURGER TIME

I *get* that you want to run away.

But couldn't you at least have a *plan*—
I can figure out what to do!

I'm not *helpless*.

You are so 18
Whatever! Like you're so brilliant!

Beatrice—
No one calls me that. It's BEA.

OK, then, Bea. I have a long trip ahead of me.
Have fun in McKinney.

SLAM

Sir! Sir. You can't sleep in here.
I'm not sleeping.

soda isn't dinner.

it's iced tea.

and technically, isn't this breakfast?
my god. You're right.

BURGER TIME

How far do you have to drive?

My great aunt is in San Angelo, which is a few days' drive away.

But I might drive more after that.
to where?
I don't know yet.

Isn't that kind of weird? To drive without... going anywhere?
I guess. I just need to... I don't know.

get out?
yeah.

yeah. exactly.

I am so stuffed
can I come with you?

I ( ) you

I...
I don't want to... just forget it.
it's late, I'm not thinking.

It's ... the drive isn't gonna be much fun.
I'm just going to West Texas.

I don't want to have fun.

well at least it'll give us a chance to work on your driving.
wait, you mean—

you ready to go?
My trailer isn't huge but I bet we'll both fit.

wait

wait, why?
why are you... I barely know you.

that's... kind of why.

everyone I know has been making me crazy. Being around someone who doesn't... who isn't...
it sounds all right.

yeah

it does to me, too.

what are you doing?
topping off the oil

we should get going. I want to get to my aunt's place in two days if we can.
kay

we'd go a lot faster with two drivers...

Bea, you-
Y'all having car trouble?

Oh, no. We're all set, thanks.

That's good to hear. I'm no good with cars but figured I'd offer my help anyways.

You happen to know any good spots for breakfast around here?
Lou! Come on, let's go.

There's Black-Eyed Susan's—'bout 20 minutes west of here. They have some fine pancakes.
But I don't know if they'll be around today.
Oh, they closed?
closed? 'Course not. They're always open.
uh
all right
thanks, then.

He was weird.
not everyone is trying to murder us, Bea.

feel for the give
first gear
slowly
What!
fuck!
Why?
I did it just like you said.
you're getting closer.

let's find some food; that'll help.
I'm terrible at this; admit it.

FIREWORKS EXIT NOW
are we in West Texas yet?

Just about. How far till the next town? There's gotta be a diner or something.
far.

There has to be something.
There's an oil refinery.

let me see the map.
it's not gonna change if you look at it.

I just want to see it.

LOOK
god
Big Spring. It's a town!
it's not on the MAP.

So what? I'm hungry.
BIG SPRING
POP: 50
EXIT NOW

None of this is how I remember it...
you've been out here a lot?

no, no. Only once before.

no.
yeah. no.

we'll just...find a place to grab and go...

MINI MART
+
GAS

there's a gas station; they'll have snacks.
no way, Lou.

Coming?
No. I'm staying here.
close the door. it's freezing.

don't you have anything warmer?
We're in Texas
it's also January.
Close the door!

Whatever. That means I get to pick your breakfast.

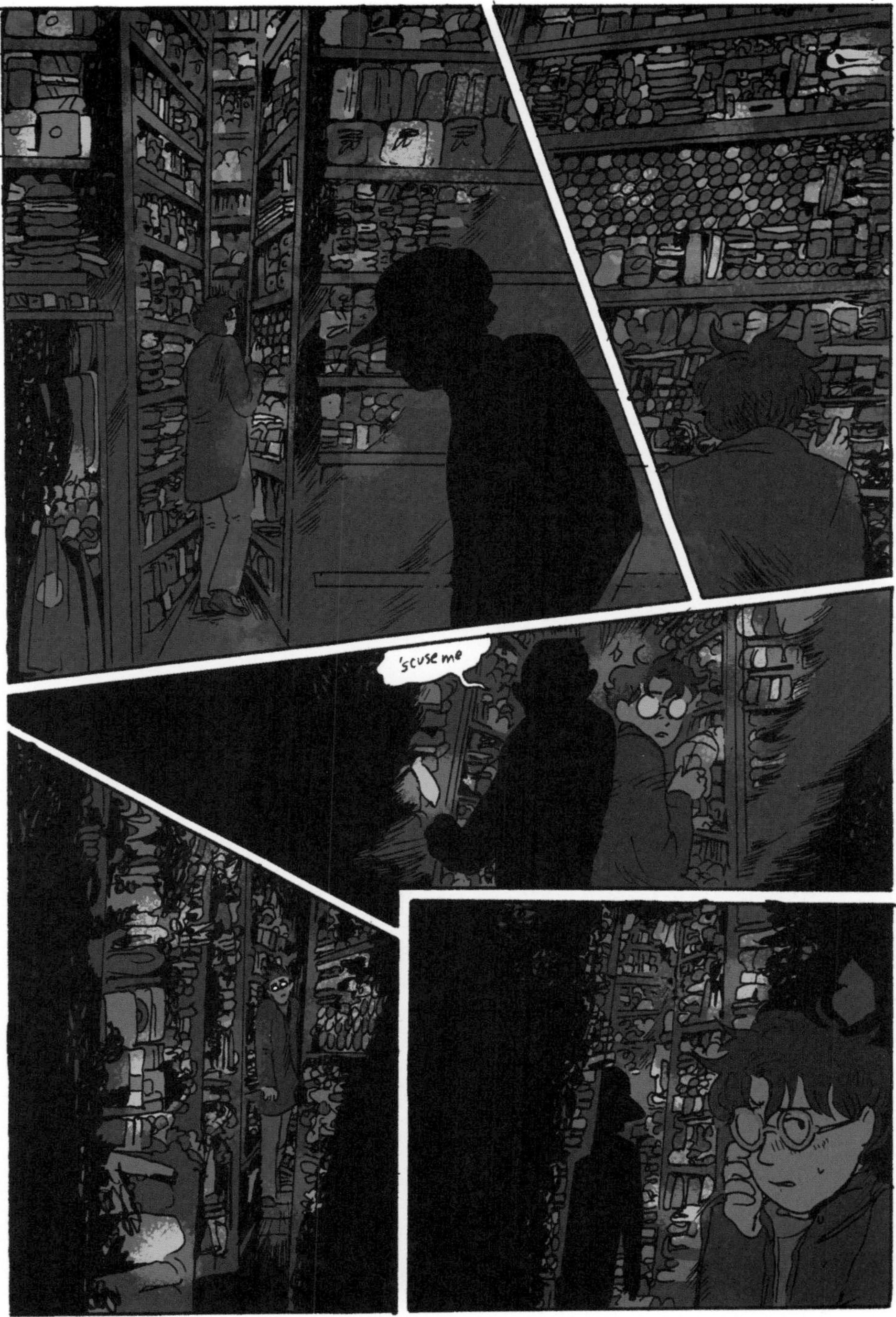
'scuse me

pardon me–

Hey!

wait!
shit
hnngh

what-

who—whose car is this?
they parked—
Hey, is this your—
Bea?
Bea?!

where did she-
ow
shitshitshit
LOU!

it's snowing! I've never...
are you okay?
Lou?
Are you-
I'm fine! I'm fine.
the store didn't make any sense and this car—
this car parked too close
I...
you can get in on my side
and slide over. It's ok.

does your chest hurt?
I... no, no.
I found her. Want to hold her?
oh my god, how much stuff did you buy?
I couldn't decide
you got chocolate rocks!
she has a tag
I tried to read it.
I can make it out... "D... 43 Glenwood Road... West, West Texas."
do you know where that is?
No...

I didn't even know there was a town called "West."
If she made it here she probably doesn't live that far...
and...
and it's really cold out.
I guess I could check out the map— see if it's on the way.
Her family is probably freaking out.
They don't know where she is.

DIAMOND
MINIMA
GAS

I got you some warmer clothes.
what?
in the bag

you didn't have to do this
you wanna check out the map?

what should we name her?
She's not our cat, Bea.
But we have to call her something.

hmm
you got me a hat?

Diamond
perfect.
HUNTER

why are you staring at me, Bea?
I'm not.
you're trying not to.

does that happen a lot?
what?
Like, getting upset and... not being able to breathe.
uh, no. I don't know. Sometimes, lately. I guess.
usually when I'm really busy I can just swallow everything down.
But without work I feel kind of... unhinged.
But... didn't you want to take this trip? Take a break?
I don't know.

you mean... you don't want to be a mechanic anymore?

No, no... I still love what I do. And that used to be enough.

Now it's... not.

Oh. uh...

Sorry, I'm rambling. Forget it.

damn.
I can't even see the road.
we gotta stop.
hopefully it'll lighten up soon.

This doesn't make any fucking sense.
you don't have to yell. I'm right here.

I'M NOT YELLING. This town doesn't exist. I've looked at every map I have.

could Diamond's tag be wrong?

I don't know. We'll have to ask someone. Maybe...
uh-huh

Bea. Would you please take a nap? You look like the dead.
I'm not tired.
bullshit.

I know you don't sleep.
you don't have to keep pretending.

I don't want to sleep.
I don't believe that.
I don't want to dream.
Are you ever gonna tell me why you're running away?
Would you stop saying that?
My mom used to make me this tea to help me sleep.
If I could find a store I could try to...
TEA isn't gonna fix this, Lou.

what's
in the
tea?

Snow's calmed down.
Come on, Bea, let's hit the road.

If we drive the rest of the day we'll get to San Angelo in the morning.

YAWN
Kay

Can you feel me accelerating?
yeah
You're gonna shift to second
I'm ready.
Now
Yes!
Can we do it again?
yeah
Hey, look...
What?
They might know where West is.
VISITOR CENTER

Come on; it's worth a shot.

HUNTER

HUNTER
WELCOME
welcome, welcome
Hi, we were just wondering if you knew anything about West? A town, I think.
West? Sure!
You know it? Is it close by?
Depends.

Lou, let's just leave.
Hold on. Could you just explain how to get there?
We found this cat, and her tag says "West."
My agency isn't responsible for dealing with the cats.
WELCOME
Lou!
I guess we can try asking my aunt. She's lived around here her whole life...

Maybe that lady was just screwing with us...
Lou! Where's Diamond!
in the grass
She's not here.
She's not?
she's probably going to the bathroom somewhere
SHIT.
We have to find her!
She's been cooped up awhile
I'm sure she's around here...
DIAMOND

DIAMOND!
Bea, relax.
Why are you so calm?
She's not even our cat.
She's lost
No one else is gonna help her, so we have to...
we have to.
I'm sure she's not far.
Let's keep looking.

mew
Bea!
mrow

I heard her
Come on
What? It's—It's too small
Uh, I'll... I'll keep watch! Or...
Bea!
It's steep. I need... I need something to hold on to.
are you
It's a tree, Lou. Not a rollercoaster.
Don't let go.

Are you ok?

Fine!

really?

Lou

Promise me we'll get Diamond home... we'll find West.

I promise.

that's disgusting!
it's literally the best.
there's a reason they sell chocolate and chips **separately**.
Look, I'll make you a perfect bite.
why do they give kids those plates with sections if not to teach us that food should not TOUCH?
Oh my god. I have so much work to do on you. Here...
ehhhh
This is the one good thing I got from my ex. She would always sprinkle salt on chocolate before eating it.
It hurts me to admit it, but she was on to something.
I didn't know that you were...
gay?
yeah.

I am, too.
yeah?
yeah.
you have a girlfriend?
what? No! God. No.
I guess it would've been weird if you'd skipped town with one.
I don't even know how I would...
like, how I would even know if they were... like me...
it's all about dropping the right clues.
but, like, HOW?
very deliberate, very gay eye contact.
LOU
Or just go up, say hi, my name is so and so...
I fuck women. What's your name?
LOU
Come on, Bea, I'm kidding. You just have to get to know someone.
UGHHH
you're crazy.
I may be crazy, but I've had three girlfriends.
Which for rural Texas is a miracle.
ok, that's fair.

was that the first time you told someone?
yeah.
you feel ok?
yeah.
did your mom know?
uh... no.
I was going to... I had a whole speech memorized...

But I had assumed she would be around when I was finally ready to...
What were you gonna say?
What?
Like, if she was here...
Why would you want—
It might help to—
Bea, that's fucked.
I just think.
No! No, god, Bea, you have no idea what you're talking about.
I'm sorry.
I know.
I'm sorry.
It's ok.
did you like it?
What?
my chocolate—potato chip combo.

it was... okay.
uh-huh, you loved it.
FOUR ACES DINER

But how did you know?
I just knew. And I didn't have time to question myself. There was too much to do.
you don't have any ideas? College or something?
mmm
don't laugh.
I always sort of wanted to... drive an ambulance.
yeah?
It'd be really fast-paced... kind of crazy.
and I'd get to wear a uniform.
I can see it.
I don't know.
we really have to work on your driving.
If everything wasn't so icy and cold I'd be doing better.
the weather makes it harder.
I didn't know Texas could get so cold...
Texas is huge; it's got room for all the heat and cold it wants.
I hate the heat. I basically spent my whole childhood inside.

Sometimes the sun was so bright it actually hurt.
yeah, it gets pretty suffocating.
My mom used to make me take walks with her every day. Rain or shine.
even when it was a zillion degrees out?
Yep.
god
yeah
But at least on those days she'd carry a cold drink with her.
The ice'd melt so fast...
come again
and when I'd start to get all red and lose my mind from the heat...she'd put the glass on the back of my neck.
it always cooled me right down.

my mom would give us ice pops...
I mean, they weren't really... it was frozen orange juice.

I would eat so many... until my throat tickled and my mouth was so cold I couldn't taste.
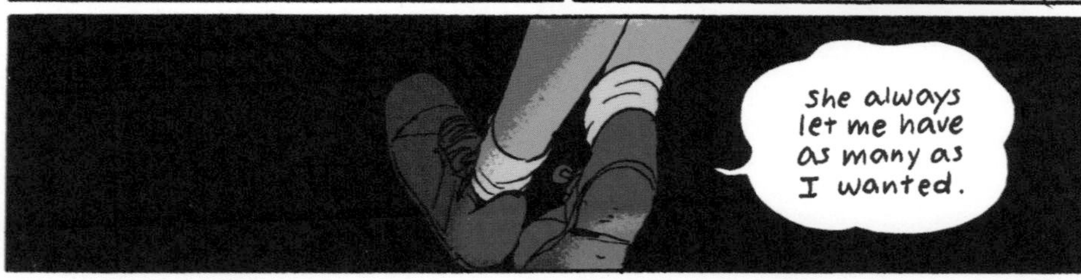
she always let me have as many as I wanted.

hah
What?

I can't even drink orange juice anymore. It makes me want to cry.

do you
we should feed Dime.
Here's the check for y'all

oh, uh, thank you
what brings y'all to these parts?

we're just passing through.
Be careful out there. 'Lotta lakes poppin' up recently.

y'all take care now

I bet D is hungry. I should look for actual cat food, probably.

You are getting hair all over my trailer bed.
prrrr

Bea?

I'm coming
FOUR ACES

shit
almost empty
GAS
EXIT NOW
1 MILE

OFFICE OF
ROAD
INQUIRY

OFFICE OF
ROAD
INQUIRY
evening, ma'am
evening
how do you do?
uh
how are ya?
no

where are my manners? My name is Bertram Tallany.
This here is Rex Whittam. We're with the Office of Road Inquiry.
Can I get your name, ma'am?

ma'am?

Sorry, fellas. I need to be on my way...

do you happen to be traveling with a feline, ma'am?

what?
no, uh, sorry. I need to get going.
SLAM

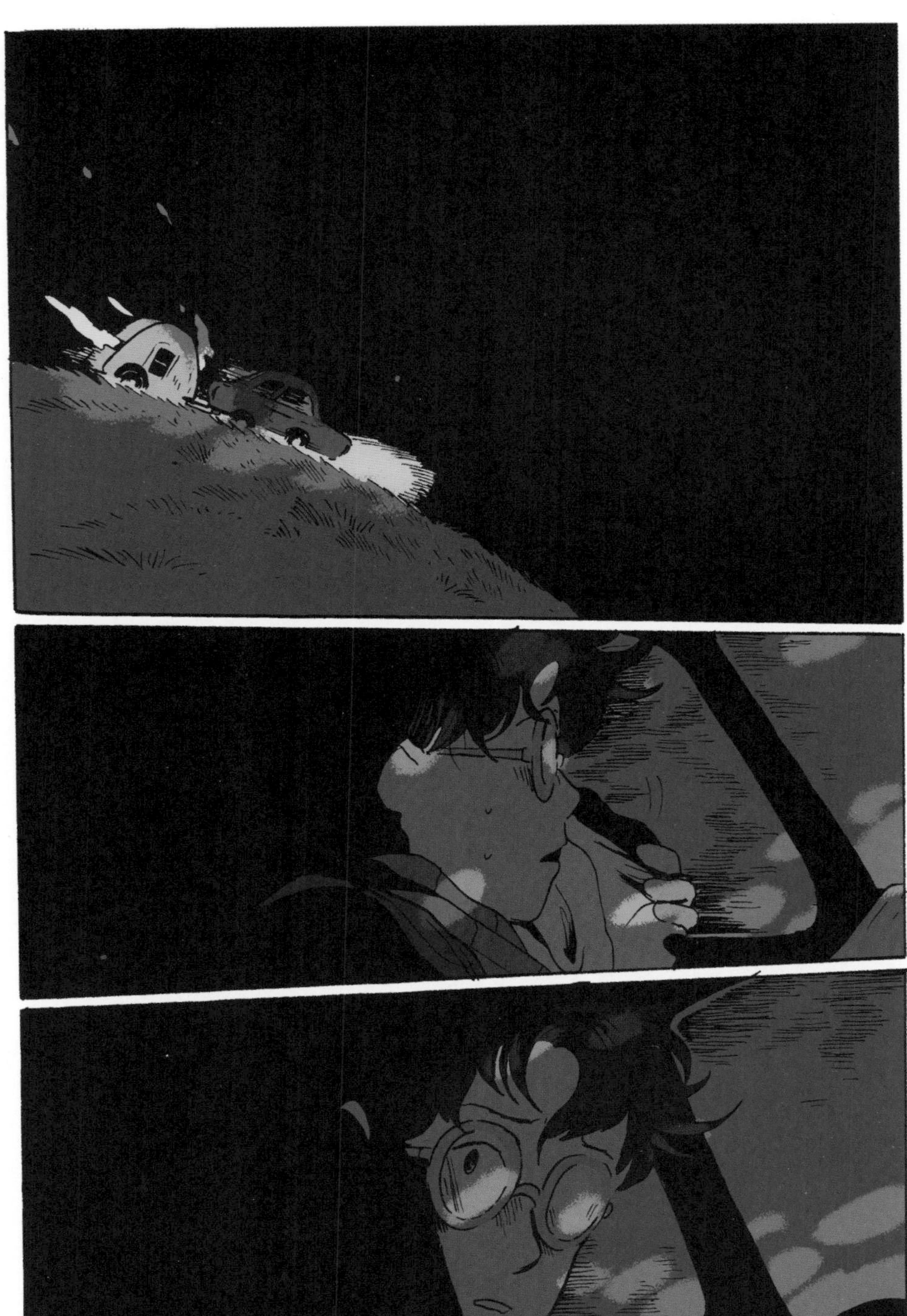

Shift up to third

LOU
damn.
we made it

does your aunt like cats?
WELCOME TO SAN ANGELO
I...really don't know.

do you know where you're going?
I'll recognize the street.

But it's been a thousand years since you've been here...

It wasn't *that* long ago; I was 13
exactly

How OLD do you think I am?

30?
WHAT? I'm 27

that's, like, basically 30.
It is NOT.

we're lost.
we're not lost.

There!

Here?
I remember this tree!

god, I'm so stiff

Lou! Is that you, honey?

How are you, Cora?
lemme get a look at you

This is my friend, Bea
Come in, Come in
Mack, get out another plate!

I remember y'all coming here when you were just a twig. Couldn't believe my eyes; you were the spittin' image of your mother.
But the second you opened your mouth I saw that was as far as the similarities went!

you were different from your mom?
we-
night and day!

Your mother was as even as even gets. No amount of chaos could phase her.

But little Lou, oh boy.

An explosive one, you were. Came in here like a tornado. You nearly broke my table when I said we were havin' jelly cake.
Now, Bea.
uh

Tell me all about you. How did you meet my Lou? What's your family like?
my dad teaches, uh, and my mom is an editor.
Ain't that nice! You got siblings?
a brother and a sister. Younger.

Tell me about yourself
There's not much to know.
Nonsense! This is Texas, honey. We don't have boring people here.

How'd you two become acquainted?
Lou lives right by us

no kidding
I worked on her mom's car a few times. And someone else in your family bought a...
wait, who?
uh... your mom's sister, I think?

she was getting a little blue Alfa for her kid. Which I guess makes him
my cousin.
right

I had a hell of a time fixing that car's engine...
San Angelo could use a mechanic like you, Lou.

the damn thing wouldn't start!

Bea?

you ok?
Bea?
God, YES, Lou. Would you back off?
you-
I'm gonna take Diamond outside. Get some air.

How you holdin' up, kiddo?
Oh, you know.
I can't believe it's been more'n a year.
I'd rather not talk about it, Cora.
Come on, D.
you hungry?
Holding it all in will only turn you gray faster.

I'm dealing with it.
I'm still just so torn up
I don't know how you could be so torn up; mom barely spent any time here.
Of course, honey. I'm not torn up for myself, I'm torn up for you.
sob

Sure I can't pack y'all anything else?
No, no, this is plenty. But if I could ask you about one more thing...
anything

Do you have any idea how to get to West?
it's a town, I think...

West? Well I sure heard of it but I couldn't tell you if it's up or down.

Whaddya need in West?
It's a long story.

I... I know West

Cross the Pecos River... drive the canyons and you'll see the sign.
You can't miss it.

: KNOCK :
: KNOCK :
Lord, they back already? Bet the rain got to be too much.
Mack, get the door!

evenin', sir.
evenin'.
mind if we ask you a few questions?

You ok if we just drive for a while? If we go all night we'll get to the Pecos at sunup.
you don't want to sleep?
not right now.
fine with me.
that tree back there... at your aunt's house...

It looked just like the tree in our front yard.
I used to climb it all the time.
uh-huh
I liked climbing it at night. It was cooler and it made the leaves and branches look all shiny.
One time... I think I was 6. I climbed all the way to the top.
I didn't know how to get down... it was so high.

I just kind of held on and panicked... but then I saw my dad through the leaves.
He was standing right by the trunk.
did he get you down?
no
I just jumped. I thought... I thought he would catch me, that he would just know I was...
But of course he didn't. I hadn't even called out to him; I just jumped.
I fell right next to him. Broke my arm.
that's horrible.

It wasn't that bad. I got a cool cast.
No, not that.
that he didn't catch you.

Bea

Bea,
wake
up

what?
it's the
Pecos
River

damn

LOU, it's
it's fine
we're not gon
we'll make it
Hold on to Diamond

See? We made it
How're we supposed to get back?

Where IS IT?
we have to be close

Mack has to be wrong
There are NO SIGNS.
ugh, I gotta take a break.
You could sleep...
yeah
...while I drive
what?
You haven't let me practice in ages!
Bea... I'm too tired...
You relax! I can do it!

fine
MOVE.

You
SHH. You're resting. I can do it.

That's it,
that's it
Keep accelerating
I'm off the road—
It's ok!
Keep going!

LOU
LOOK

TOWN OF
WEST

will you
yeah

Lou

I see it

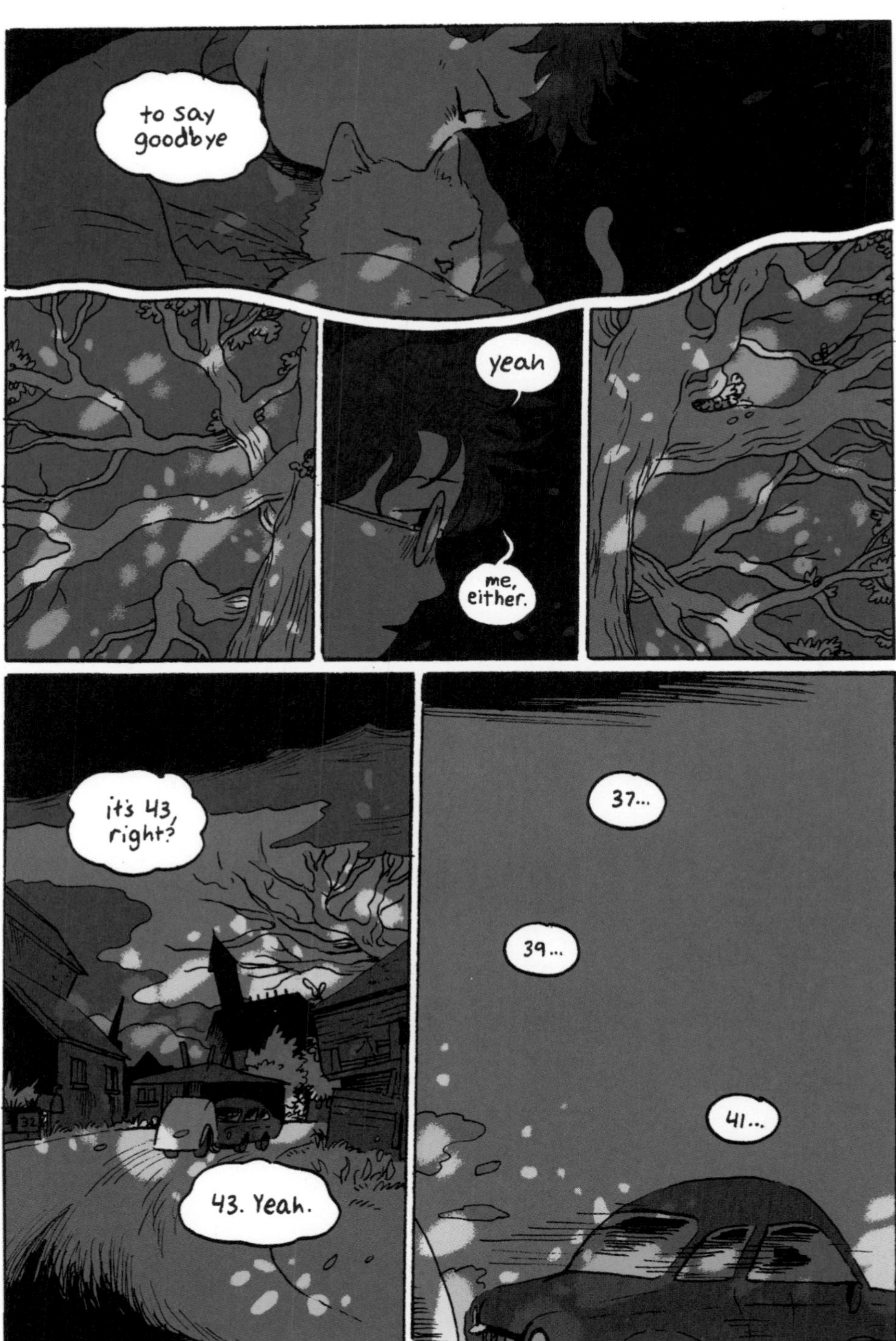
to say goodbye
yeah
me, either.
it's 43, right?
43. Yeah.
37...
39...
41...

43

FUCK

of course,
of course.
well, this has been great. We came all this way for a fucking TREE.
I'm done, I'm so done.
I don't even know what I'm doing out here.
Come on, Bea.
we're going back. It's time for me to go home.
I gotta get back to work.
I can't keep wandering around. Jesus, what is wrong with me?
Bea.

we just...
we just have to find the main road...

Then we can start tracing our way back... FUCK, Why is it SNOWING
If there were any cars around we could ask for directions.
is that-
Finally! A car!

HEY!
excuse me
HEY
row
OFFICE OF ROAD INQUIRY
Oh, shit

How did they even
afternoon, ma'am.
mind if we have ourselves a little chat?
I'm afraid we didn't get through everything the last time we found ourselves together.

what?
Sorry, boys. We don't have anything for you. We're gonna be on our way.
Lou
Bea, get in the car
What are...
Shit! Don't let them see-
Why, that is one fine kitty you've got there.
sure is.

OW
LOU
What is going ON?

shit, they're following us
WHAT?

are we criminals? Are we being chased by the police?
WHAT? They're not after ME!
wait, what
Oh, no, Bea, not you, they—
I think they want Diamond...
they... what? Why?
I don't know!
you don't know?
NO.

They... They came up to me a few days ago and asked if we had a cat and... I didn't tell them. They were... something felt off...
Why didn't you tell me?
I don't know! I didn't—
shit
they're right—

Lou, they're—
I KNOW
Lou, BREATHE
I can tell you're holding your breath!
I'll lose 'em

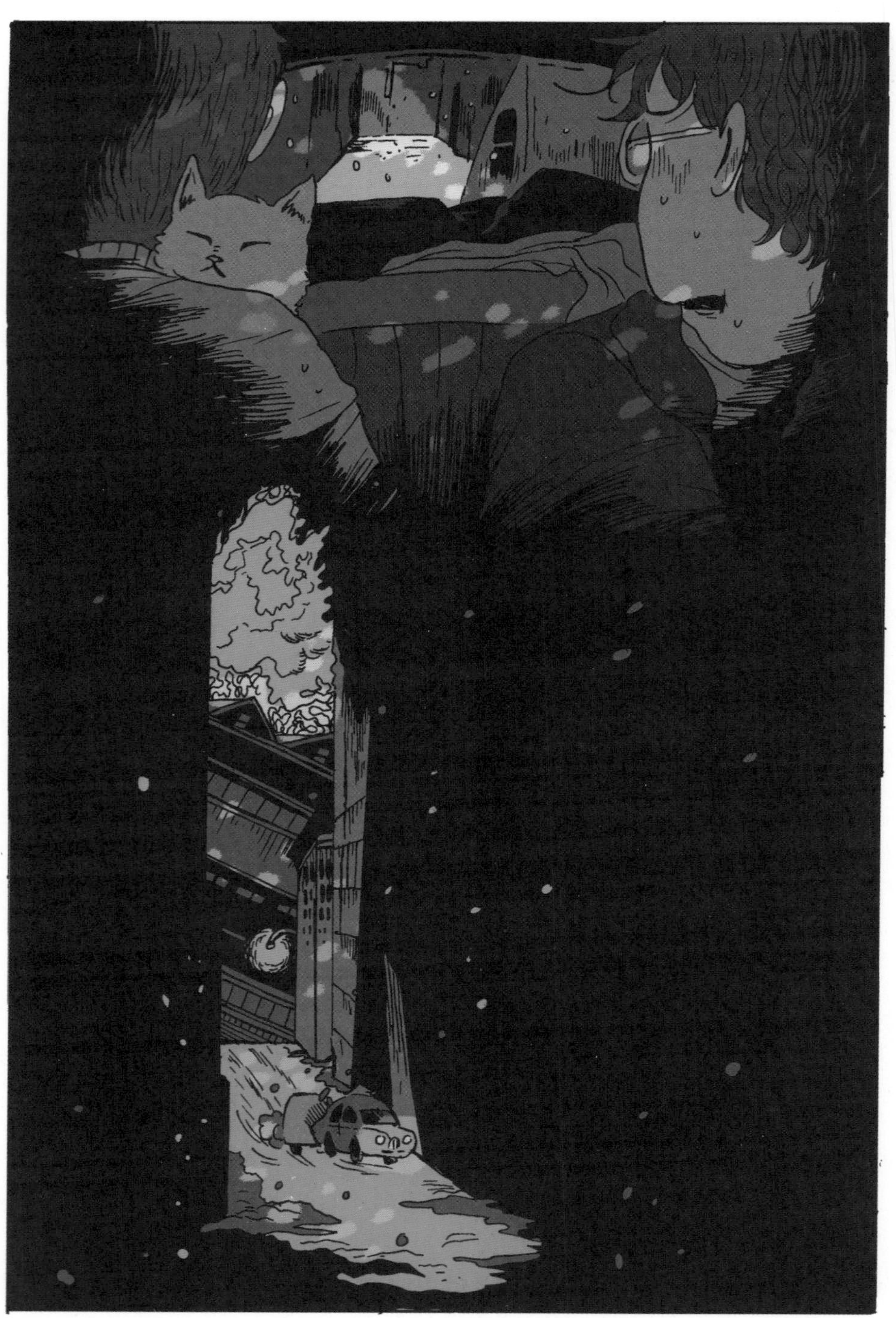

I don't see them
I think we lost them
Why do they want Diamond?

I have no idea.
they're not gonna get her.

no, they're fucking not.

any sign of them?
no.

when I was a kid, we used to play this game...
well, it wasn't really much of a game, now that I think about it.

this girl Sophie would go up in her tree house and throw a ball down to us...
...whoever caught it won and got to go up to the tree house with her.

and I never got the ball. It drove me crazy.
Finally, we were playing one time and my friend Alex caught it.
And it was like I snapped. I walked over and attacked her.
Pulled the ball from her hands while she cried.
and you know what's horrible?
I felt relieved. I was... I was finally gonna get to go in the tree house.

But... it ended up not mattering.
What do you mean?

Oh... Sophie came down, called me Crazy. Then let everyone go into the tree house except me.

It was so humid that day.
prrrr

Lou
we should find a place to stop.

we don't even know where we are.

We can get some sleep and I'll look at the map for a good route home.

You promised we'd get D home!
We tried! And, these guys, all this **shit**—

But—
it's not **safe**, and I'm not gonna get us killed over a **cat**.
We're not—
and, and your parents are probably freaking out!

they don't know where you are and I feel like I kidnapped you, and we're wasting time
it's time to go **home**.

row

you don't know anything
What—
you're an asshole

Oh I'm an asshole? I'm the one who's been ferrying you around for no reason.
I could be lost or alone or—
or getting chased by fucking monsters who eat cats
and I'd still be safer than I would be at home.
hnn
:sniff:
:sob:

ok
ok
I'm not gonna let anything happen to you.

you hungry?
not really.
come on, Bea. Let's get some real sleep.

where are we...?
I...don't know.
It just seemed kind of hidden.

far from the main road.
Diamond!

where is she...
D, it's sleep time!

Lou, she's-
Diamond! NO!

god DAMMIT, Diamond, haven't you put us through ENOUGH?
Dimey

It's kind of tight in here...
suck it up
DIAMOND

Is she-
I saw her tail

she went
in here

the water is... warm...

here
I didn't have towels but this'll work.

I thought...

I thought getting far away would fix everything.

and it fixed some stuff, but...
at home, it was like one huge cut inside me.
and now it's...
it's like it broke into pieces, thousands of pieces...
I gave my parents this whole story. A job, a friend, I can't even remember.
did they buy it?
my dad did.
my mom saw right through me

She could tell I wasn't gonna come back
She just... started crying. Begged me to stay and talk to her
and I left. I walked out while she... she...
I felt like a monster
Why did you have to go?

because he
would've kept
doing it
he
don't
don't say that
word. I hate it.
who
is he?

promise you won't think I'm disgusting
No!
No.
I would never think that.
my cousin
we grew up together. He lived 5 minutes away...
our birthdays are a week apart

maybe there were signs, but I never
I never imagined he could...
it was just a normal day. Like them all... I was wearing my red t-shirt.
he said...
he said he was gonna show me how to wrestle
everyone was downstairs.
I could hear them laughing
moving chairs
that was the first time
I had no idea what was happening

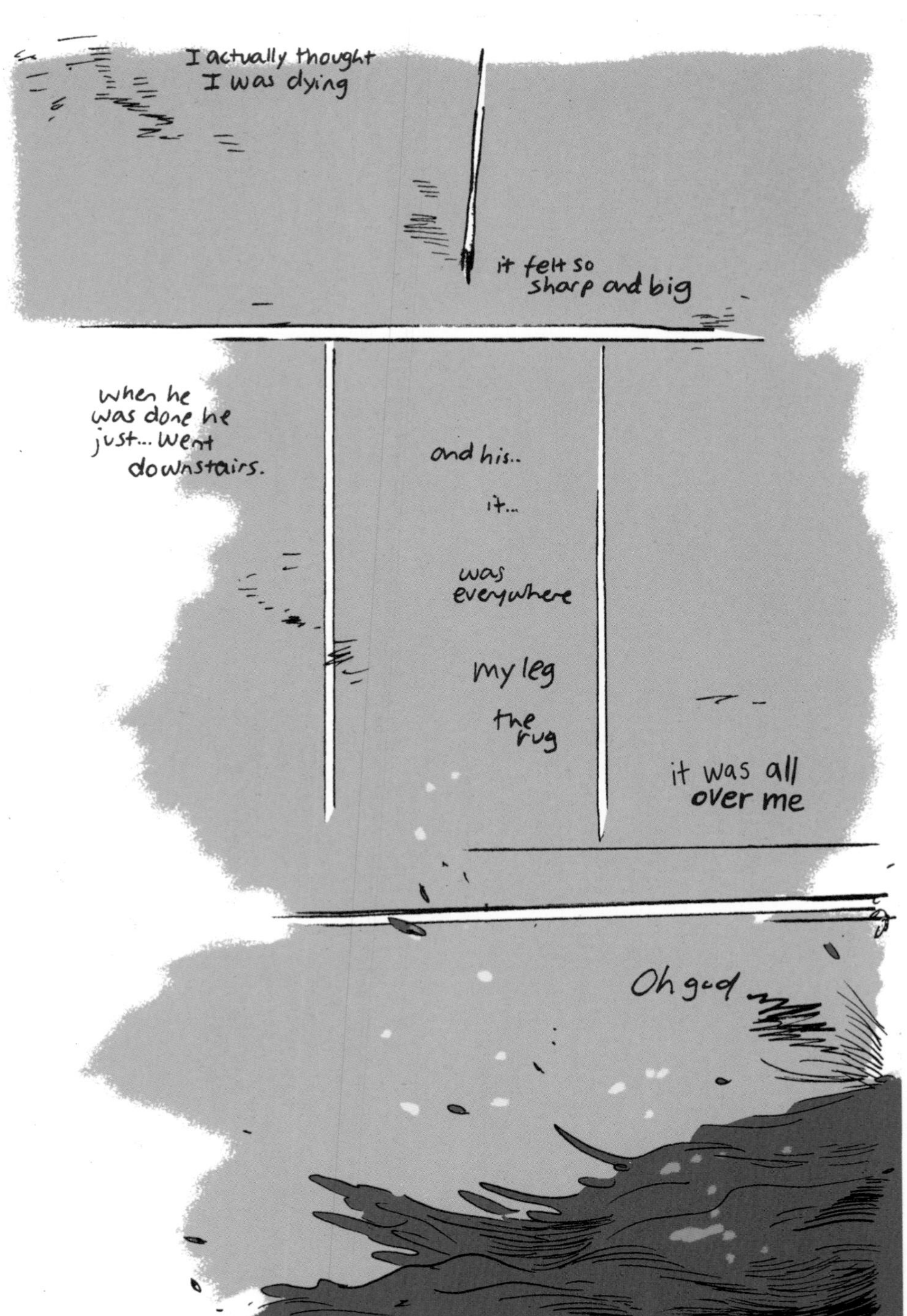
I actually thought I was dying
it felt so sharp and big
when he was done he just... went downstairs.
and his..
it...
was everywhere
my leg
the rug
it was all over me
Oh god

my little sister came to get me for dinner
and I screamed at her. For no reason.
She...she's scared of me now.
but I...
I didn't mean it
I know
I was just scared for her
I know
I know
did you ever tell-
who is there to tell? We're related, He-they-
they would never forgive me

forgive? you've- you've done nothing wrong, you
yeah right
it kept happening!
He kept coming back and-and
I didn't fight back
you did fight. You left. you got out of there. you-
I should've screamed! I should've clawed his fucking eyes out
You told me. you told me.
That's fighting.

it's not your fault
Bea
are you listening?
none of this is your fault

I'm so tired, Lou.

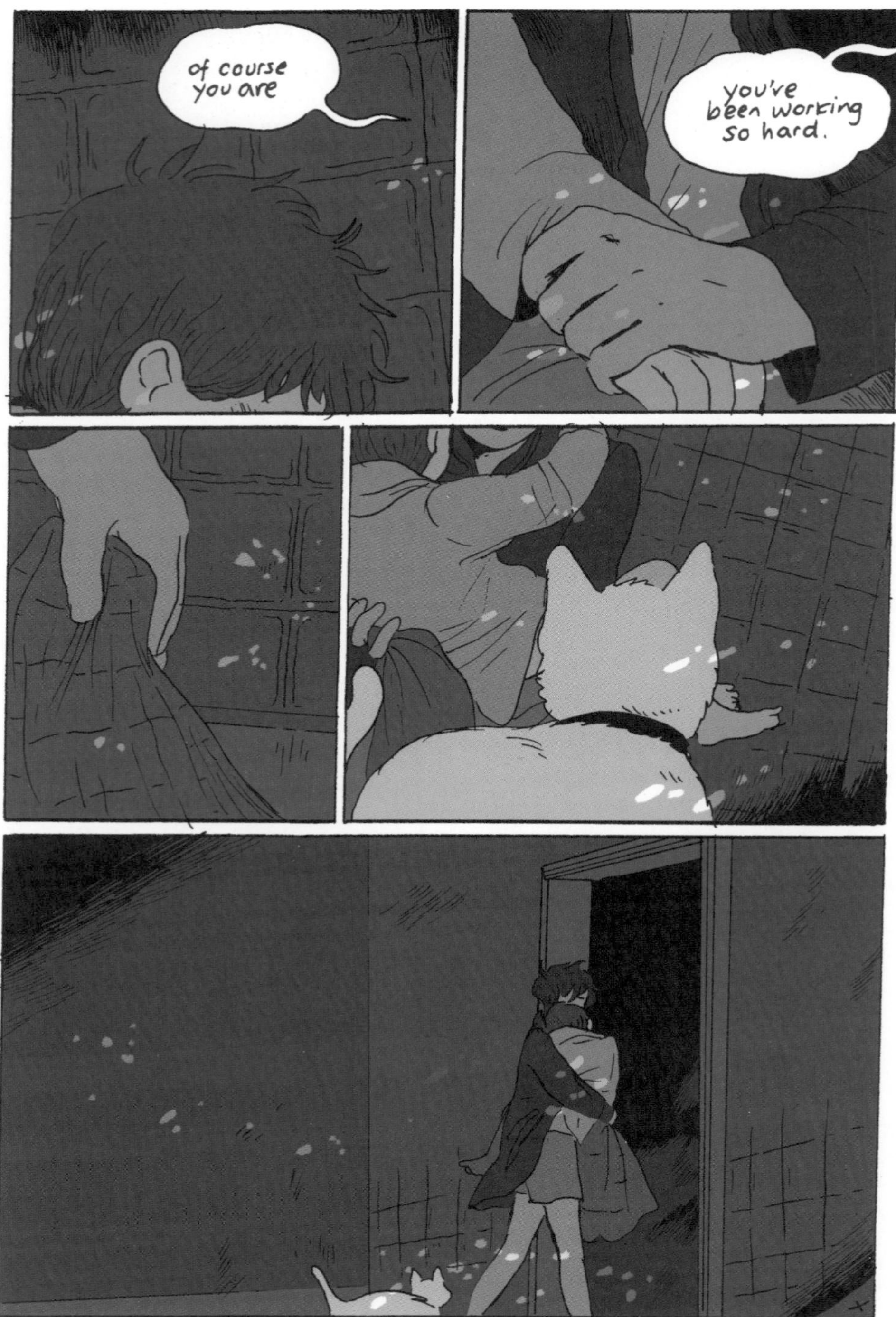
of course you are
you've been working so hard.

creeeakk

Hey there, darlin'.

mmm
I'm so done with this.
let's get real, boys

Dimey, stop
what do you want with our cat?
and let me just say this is purely out of curiosity.
you're not getting her.
we're not at liberty to answer, ma'am
it's a matter of transportation safety
ok. Here's what's gonna happen.

I'm gonna drive away, and you're gonna find someone else to stalk.
cool? cool.
unfortunately we can't accept that, ma'am.
row
row
row
what?
this matter is of interest not only to the Office of Road Inquiry but also to the Division of Highway Bridges and Culverts and it is necessary for us to involve ourselves in accordance with the Federal Road Act.

FINE, fine.
I'm up.
Happy?
LOU!

THE CAT
Bea! Get in the car!
Bea!

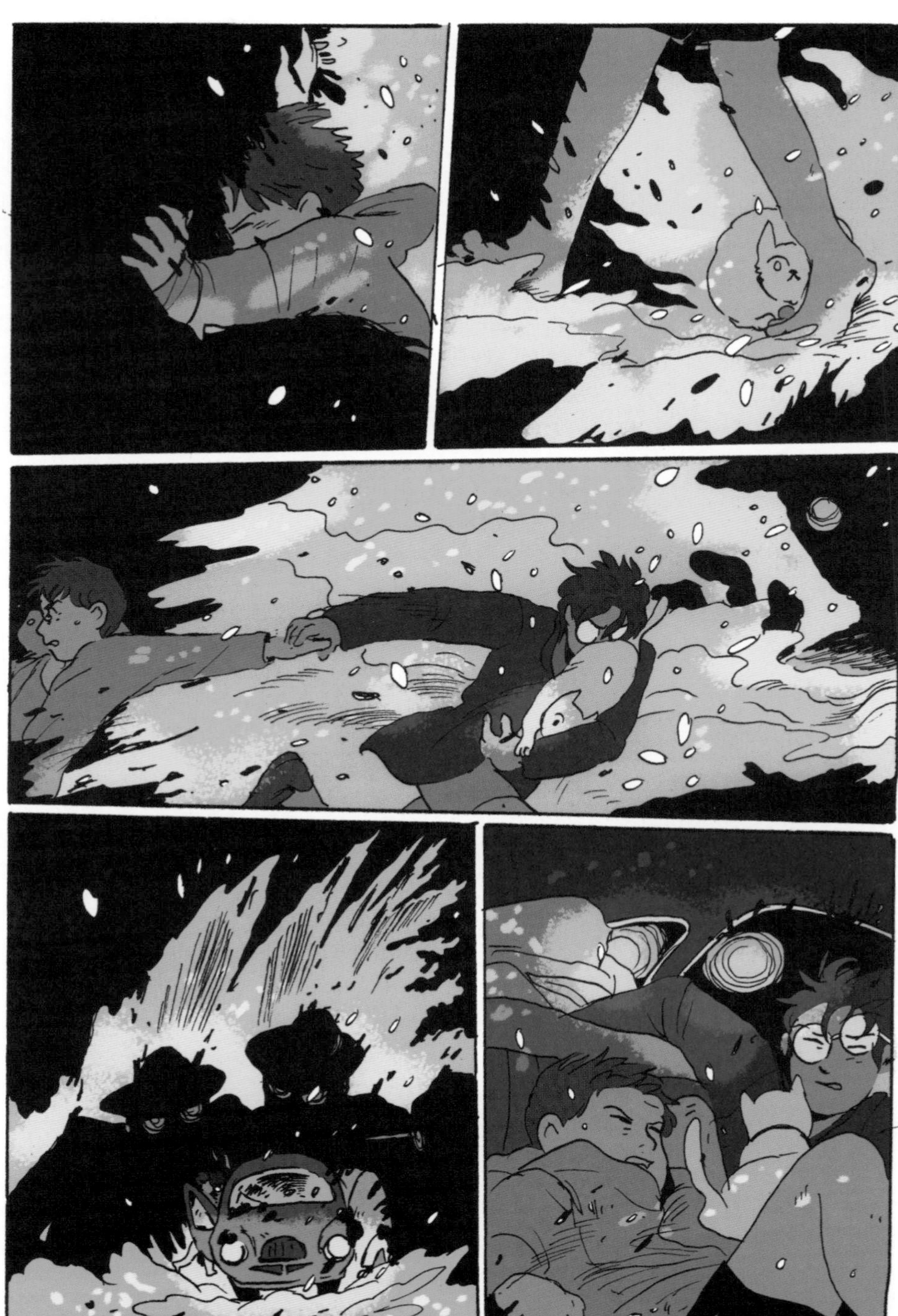

we're...
we're fucked.

There...
There has to be a way out.
hnnn
There's nowhere to go, girls.
Lou
I can't, Bea
Lou, drive.
prrr
Bertram, be a good fellow, get me my wrench.
DRIVE

How
JUST GO
Get in the vans! NOW
the damn cat figured it OUT

don't slow down!
I-

This car can't handle these kinds of hills
they're catching up!
GO FASTER!
I can't

it's overheating. we have to stop
your car matters more to you than us?
THIS was my mom's car! It was OURS
I won't let anything—

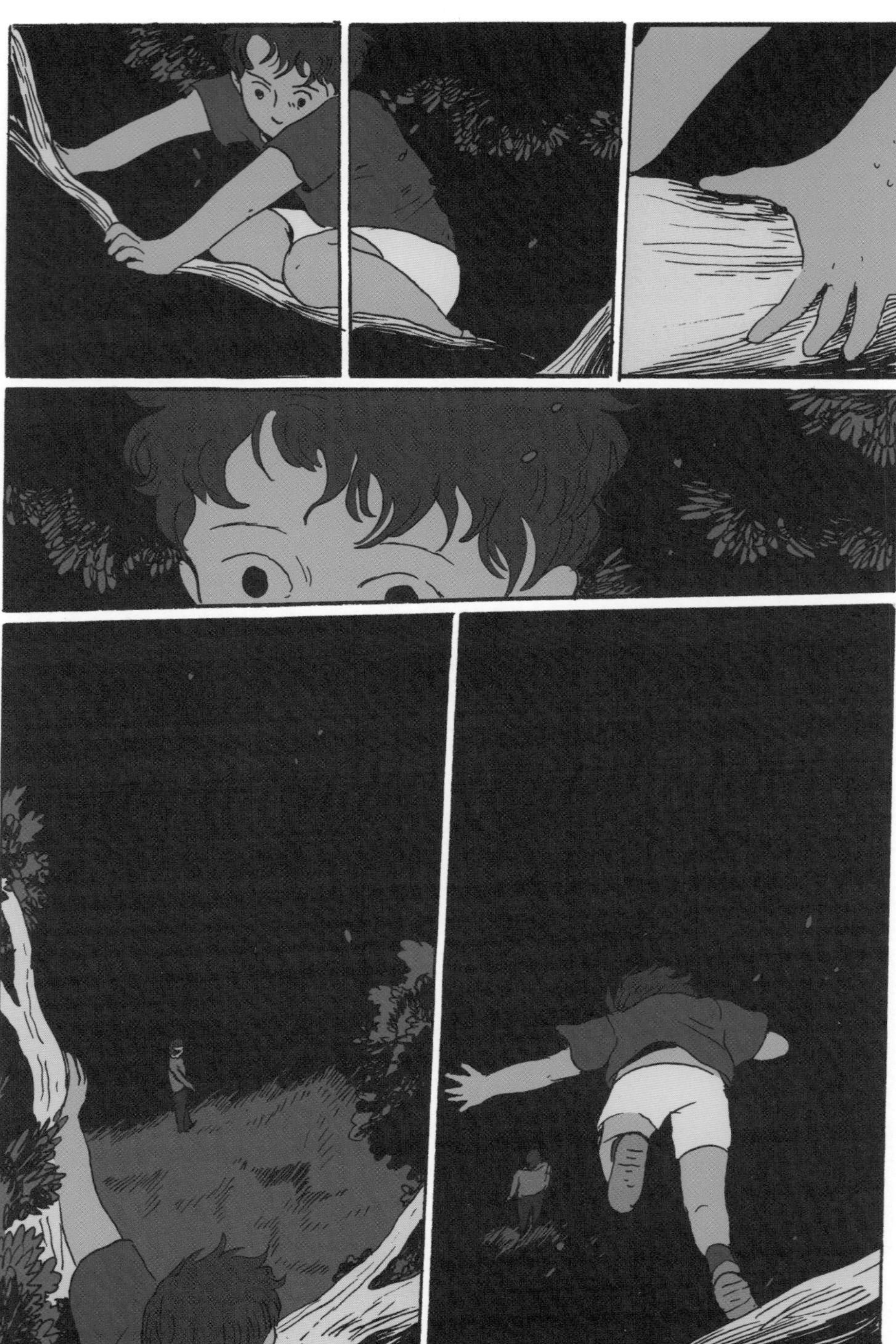

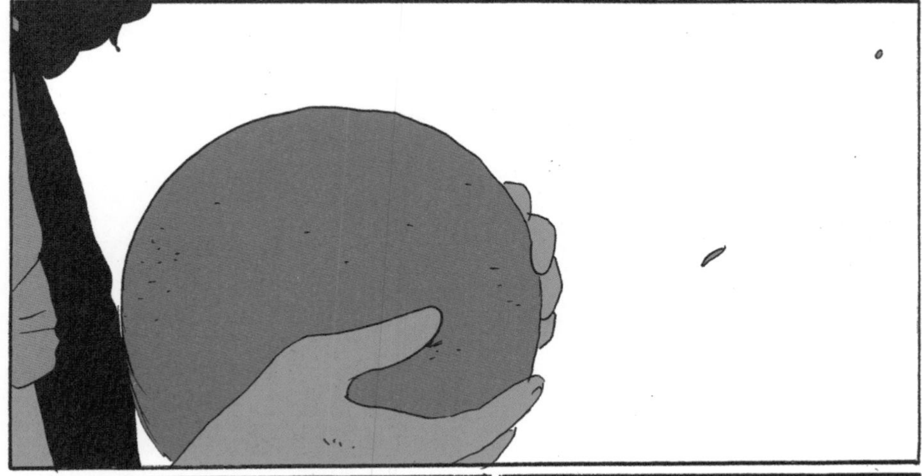

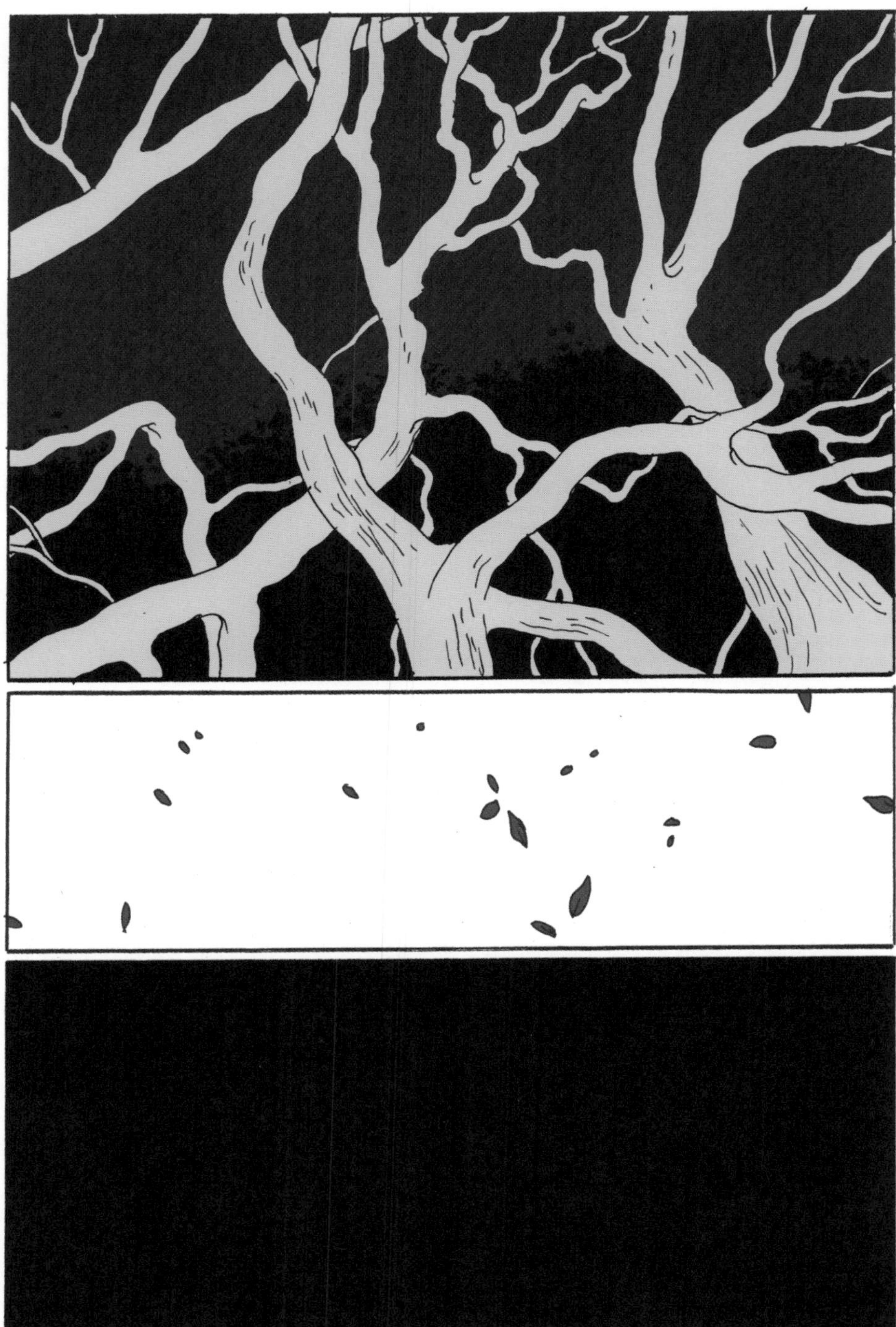

OW
Shit
Lou?
LOU, where are you?
LOU

I knew it.
I knew it
I told her all... of course she wants nothing to do with me...
mew
DIAMOND?
DIMEY
meow

Diamond
your leg...
it's ok,
it's ok.
mow
Im gonna find you some help, ok?
we don't need Lou.
we're ok.
we're ok.

LOU
LOU

we just... we just gotta find the road...
row
hang in there, D.

oh, god
I need...
I need help...

TOWN OF...
WEST

WOOD RD
LEWELLYN RD
43

:KNOCK:
:KNOCK:

Hello?

HELLO?

I have your cat

About time you got here.
Come on in.

is...is this your cat? Am I... in the right place?

of course.
Her address is on her tag.

I... she's hurt. I'm so sorry.

bring her here

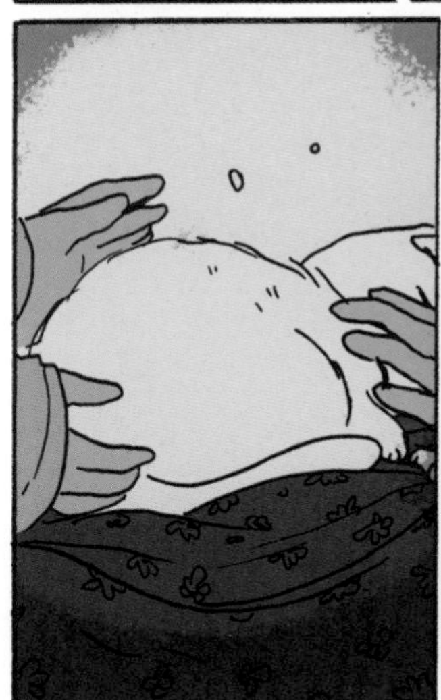

hmm

she'll be ok.

what's going on? None of this makes any sense.
why do those guys want her?
you mean she hasn't shown you what she can do?

I mean... sort of. She... she saved us, I think.
I know she's special.
I can feel it.
oh, she's just a regular cat.
you don't believe me?
no.
cats are sensitive critters.
They take the cue of where they are.
Take her somewhere typical, well, most she'll ever do is sleep.
But out here...
well, West Texas is the perfect blend of giant and tiny.
The land, the sky... it's got its own mind
its own heart.

she just taps into that.
out here, building a road is as easy for her as rolling on her back.
but... if it's not just her, it's the place, does that mean...
of course. Everyone, everything has potential for magic.
you just gotta be standing somewhere in the world and in the body that lets you see it.
how have you kept her safe?
they really want her.
they sure do. We don't have many cats out here, and even fewer roads.

luckily those road boys aren't too bright. They're just insistent.
The fact that they can't control everything that moves only makes 'em try harder.
you're not scared of them?
I try not to be. Lucky for us, they haven't spent any time gettin' to know the land they want so desperately.
Texas is water.
And the Office of Road Inquiry treats it like a place they can grab and hold forever.
we'll always slip right through their fingers.
But how... how can a place be... It's solid! It doesn't change!

when something horrible happens, or something amazing... really, anything that's **big**, it makes you feel like mountains could shatter, or the sky could disappear...
you know what I'm talking about?
yes.
Well, most places, mountains stay put. Sky stays in one piece. Kind of cruel, really.
But here, everything is listening.
the roads, the clouds, the trees... they know all your secrets.
everything you've seen is built by you.
which is why you'll never see it again.

that's bullshit. If that were true then everything around me would be on fire because that's how I feel.
if that were the case, then we'd smell smoke.
Some part of you is still solid because, well...
everything is still here.

Can I...
Can I ask you something?
Bea!
my friend... she... I don't...
I don't know where she is and I...
I don't know how to help her

BEA?
here's what you need to know.

no
no
fuck
BEA
DIAMOND

shit

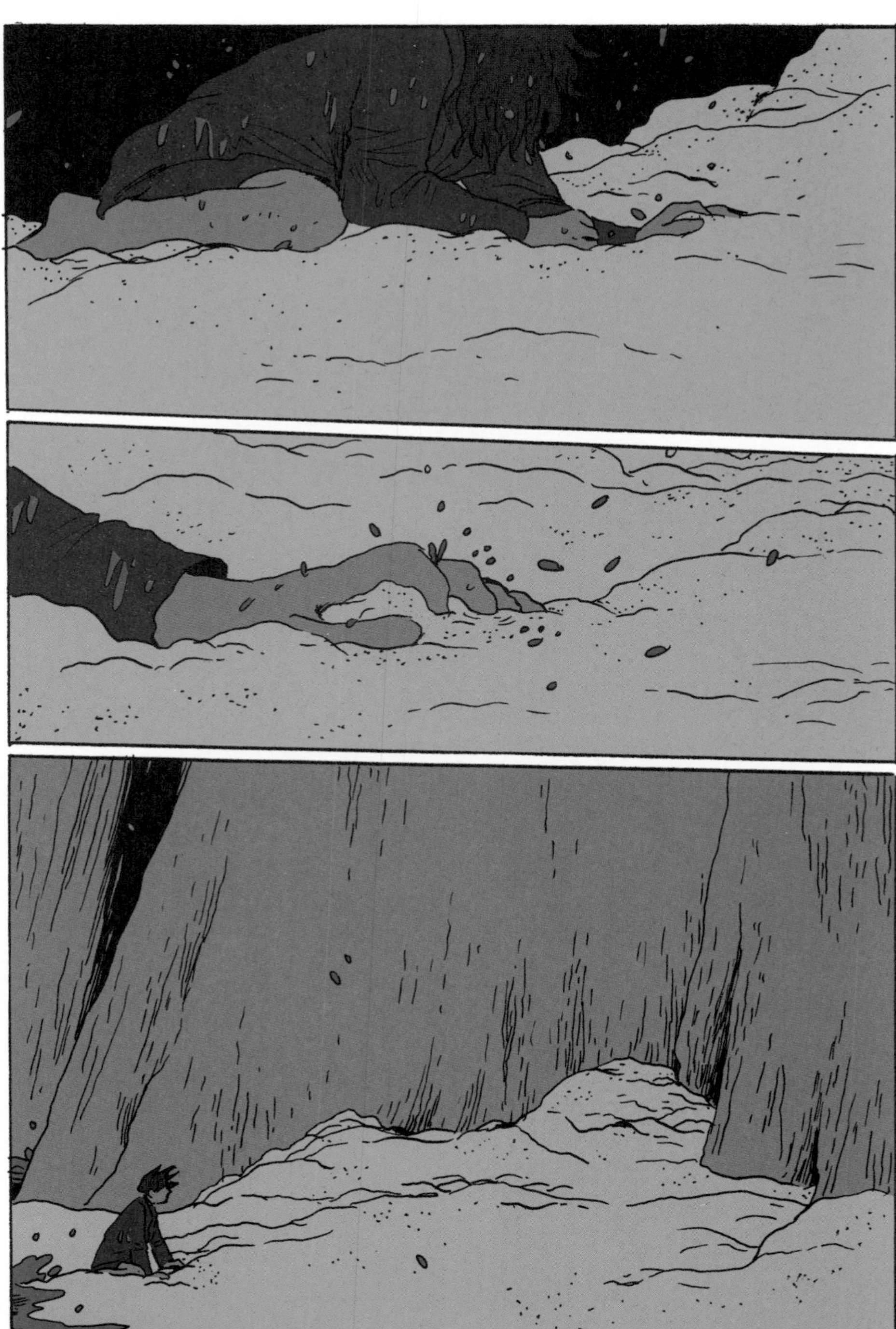

It's not fair
It's not...
I want you to know who I am now
I want you to see that I grew up
and that I cut my hair

you would've known how to help her
she's just a kid
she's just...

I miss you
So much I want
to throw up.

Mom.

MOM.

it's too hot out.
mhmm
can't we skip today? we could walk twice tomorrow...
we have to, Lou.
we have to move every day.
even when we don't want to.

THAT'S STUPID.
This is stupid.
Come here, baby.

Let me cool you down.
See?
Isn't that better?

I'm coming for you, Bea.
I'm Coming.

it's hard to say goodbye.
She...she made me feel really safe, which I know is strange to say after everything...
I won't forget you, D.

You can use my old bike. It's around the back
How will I find her?
That's a question you'll need to answer on your own.
don't worry.
you'll be back here someday.

LOU

Lou, I need you

GAS ST
COFFEE · S
2 M

excuse me, do y'all have maps?

Over here
DING

oh thank god

orange
CHOCO-YUM
So, she's ok?
She's home.

When I...
When I couldn't find you or Diamond...

I thought...

ever since my mom died, it feels like anything can happen.

I wish I could go back to believing there were things that weren't possible.

Lou

She told me stuff about you.
About your mom.

do you want to know what she said?

...

ISLAND
MOTEL
VACANCY

Diamond wasn't very noisy.
but it's quieter without her, somehow.
yeah.
Bea
tomorrow...
I know.
It's been a good trip.

yeah.
a good trip.
TEXAS

DIAMOND

LOU
what do you see behind us?
what?
it's just... a lot of land

you must be joking.
ma'am.
BILLS USED CARS
I'm not paying that.

I...I suppose
I could
do you
know who
you're
talking to?

I'm a mechanic.
A damn good one.
You can't pull any
tricks on me.
uh

Lou, that
took forever!

guy nearly pissed himself. Got it for a steal.
Your bus'll be here any minute!

Shit, I won't have time to show you...
It's in the alley!
I'll figure it out. Come on!

you sure about this?
yeah. I need a break from driving.
This way I'll be able to close my eyes...
...and open them when I'm home.
Besides, I'll need the rest. The second I'm back I'm gonna work so hard I'll puke.
can you give this to my mom?
for Mom from Bea

of course.

when you're ready to come home... if you ever want to...
you come stay with me. You're always welcome.

y'all gettin' on?

will you be ok? I don't have to—
you do. Go.

wherever you land, get your driver's license, ok?

you'll ace the test.

process...

Saab 96
1961
column shift
3 speed
3 cylinder
2 stroke
engine
B gets not on the bus
who is it?
give them a reason to
get together
Lu is at beginning
and I know the ending of
this fucking book
huzzah!
need to create interesting places to
make mayhem
get caught up in plot?
I. dont
want to leave yet

1st attempt at pencils

2nd go...

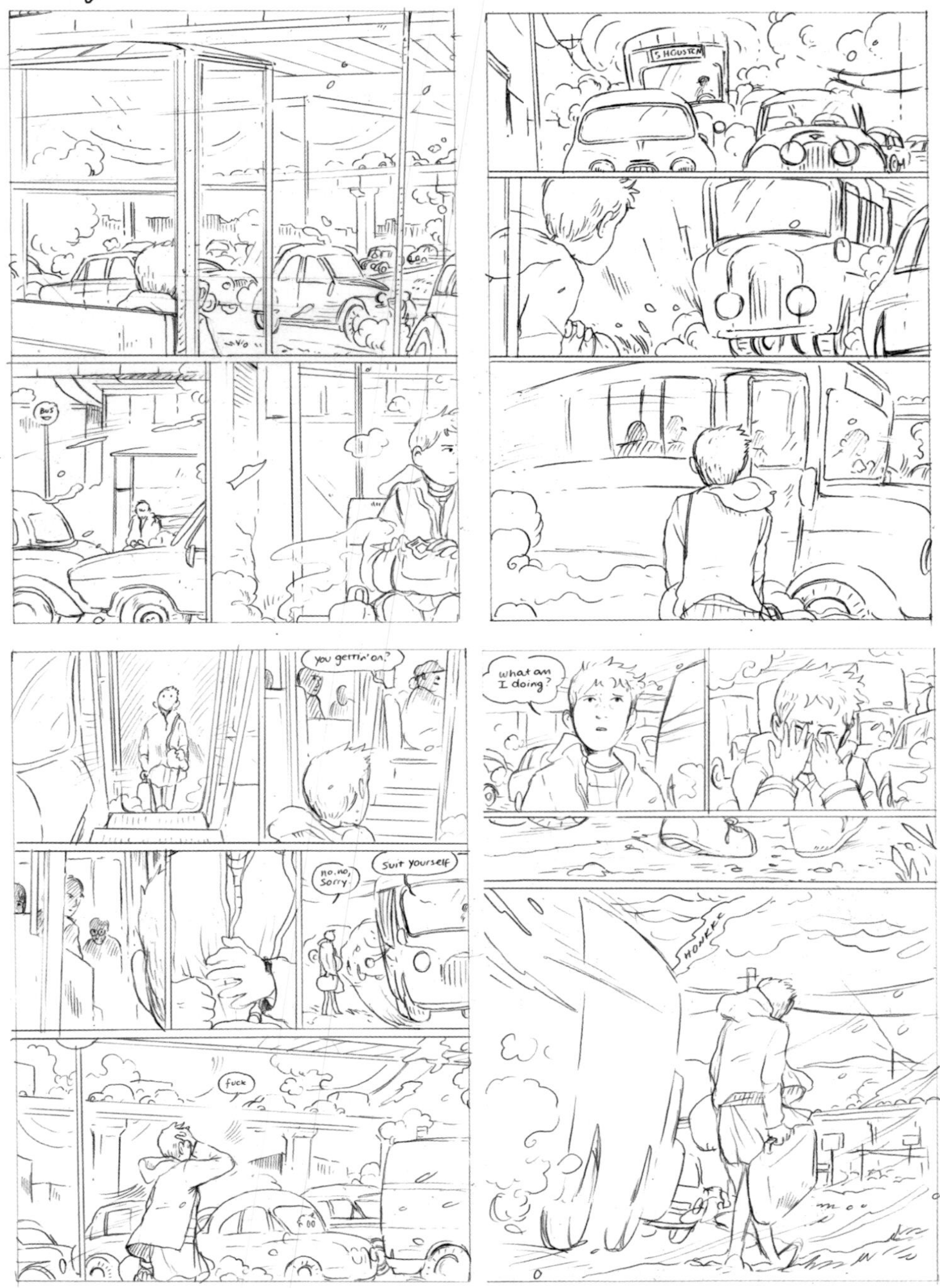

S HOUSTON
BUS
you gettin' on?
no, no, sorry
suit yourself
fuck
what am I doing?
HONKK
moo

Inking...

acknowledgments

there were many times working on this book that I wanted to give up. It was the support of people around me that got me through it. I like to think that I have some sort of never-ending well of energy and time and that it is through sheer grit that I manage to make long books in short times. But this is so far from the truth. I am still here because of those of you who continue to support me and love me. Here are some of those people:

my First Second family. All of you who have touched this book and helped it get here.

Connie, my dear editor, who never gives up on me.

Seth, who values me more than I value myself.

My roommate and assistant, Annamarie, who kept me fed and alive while making this book.

Jarad, who flatted this book in miraculous time and helped me make it beautiful.

my family, whose support is more vast than I can describe.

And of course, to you, for listening to what I had to say.

-t

Praise for Tillie Walden

A.V. Club Best Book of the Year
Paste Best Book of the Year
Wired Best Comic of the Year

"This beautiful story about sorrow, growth, and triumph will resonate in every reader's heart."
—**Laurie Halse Anderson**, author of *Speak*

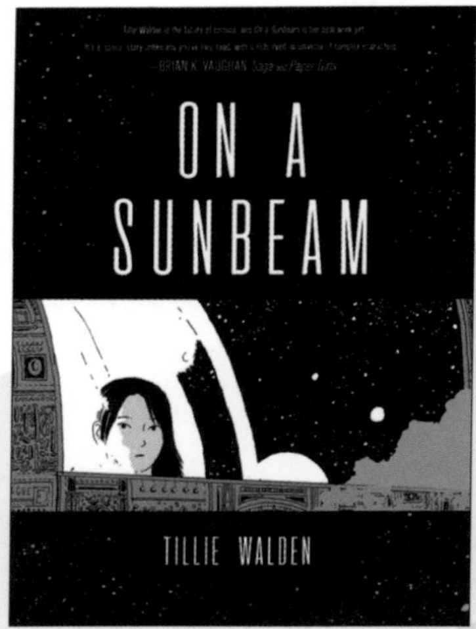

A.V. Club Best Book of the Year
A *Washington Post* "10 Best Graphic Novels of 2018"
A Chicago Public Library "Best of the Best 2018"

"Tillie Walden is the **future of comics**, and *On a Sunbeam* is her best work yet. It's a 'space' story unlike any you've ever read, with a rich, lived-in universe of complex characters.""

—**Brian K. Vaughan**,
author of *Saga* and *Paper Girls*

Tillie Walden is a cartoonist and illustrator from Austin, Texas. She is the creator of the graphic memoir *Spinning*, an Eisner Award winner, and *On a Sunbeam*, which was originally published as a webcomic. She is also the creator of the Ignatz Award winner *The End of Summer* and *I Love This Part*. Tillie is a graduate of the Center for Cartoon Studies, a comics MFA program in Vermont.

tilliewalden.com

I LOVE GRAPHIC NOVELS!

Keep reading with these amazing books.

I want a book that's excitement and magic from start to finish!

Please give me the most possible adventures.

Apocalyptic adventures!

LAST PICK
JASON WALZ

Otherworldly adventures!

Historical adventures!

Magical stories FTW!

Magic and myth and self-acceptance!

Magic and family and identity!

I want a book that's thoughtful and realistic!

Absolutely true stories!

About amazing women throughout history!

BRAZEN
REBEL LADIES WHO ROCKED THE WORLD
PÉNÉLOPE BAGIEU

About ice skating, first love, and coming out!

Books belong in the kitchen.

Pie and hockey and more pie!

CHECK, PLEASE!
NGOZI UKAZU

Bakery disasters and boyfriends!

The best books are kissing books!

Especially when you can kiss in gorgeous dresses!

The PRINCE and the Dressmaker
Jen Wang

Especially when there's dramatic family history!

KISS NUMBER 8

First Second
firstsecondbooks.com